Echo and the Bat Pack

THE CHILLY MAMMOTH

text by Roberto Pavanello
translated by Marco Zeni

STONE ARCH BOOKS
a capstone imprint

First published in the United States in 2013
by Stone Arch Books
A Capstone Imprint
1710 Roe Crest Drive
North Mankato, Minnesota 56003
www.capstonepub.com

Text by Roberto Pavanello
Original cover and illustrations by Blasco Pisapia and Pamela Brughera
Graphic Project by Laura Zuccotti and Gioia Giunchi

© 2008 Edizioni Piemme S.p.A., via Tiziano 32 - 20145 Milano- Italy
International Rights © Atlantyca S.p.A., via Leopardi, 8 — 20123 Milano, Italy — foreignrights@atlantyca.it

Original Title: IL MAMMUT FREDDOLOSO

Translation by: Marco Zeni

www.batpat.it

LIbrary of Congress Cataloging-in-Publication Data is available on the Library of Congress website.

Library Binding: 978-1-4342-3835-1
e-book PDF: 978-1-4342-4626-4

Summary: Echo and the Bat Pack make a "chilling" discovery when they uncover a real, live woolly
mammoth!

Designer: Emily Harris
Production Specialist: Michelle Biedscheid

Printed in the United States of America in North Mankato, Minnesota.
042012   006682CGF12

TABLE OF CONTENTS

Hello there!

I'm your friend Echo, here to tell you about one of the Bat Pack's adventures!

Do you know what I do for a living? I'm a writer, and scary stories are my specialty. Creepy stories about witches, ghosts, and graveyards. But I'll tell you a secret — I am a real scaredy-bat!

First of all, let me introduce you to the Bat Pack. These are my friends. . . .

Becca

Age: 10

Loves all animals (especially bats!)

Excellent at bandaging broken wings

Michael

Age: 12

Smart, thoughtful, and good at solving problems

Doesn't take no for an answer

Tyler

Age: 11

Computer genius

Funny and adventurous, but scared of his own shadow

Dear fans of scary stories,

Are you interested in paleontology? Do you know what it is? Don't worry if you don't. I didn't either, at least until the Bat Pack and I went on our latest adventure.

That's when I discovered that paleontologists are scientists who explore the most remote corners of the earth looking for the fossils of extinct animals. When they find fossils, the paleontologists become famous, just like the paleontologist who discovered the oldest fossil of a prehistoric bat! I can't quite remember his name. Jack, or John, or . . . oh, well.

It'll come to me by the end of my story.

I'm sure I've mentioned before that I am not a fan of cold weather. Not one bit. Cold weather makes my ears freeze, which is especially terrible since we bats need our ears very badly. Why is this important, you ask? Because on our most recent adventure, the Silver kids and I ended up in one of the coldest places on earth! It was completely covered with snow and ice and colder than I could have ever imagined!

If I had known where we were going ahead of time, I would have put on a fur coat, a pair of boots, and maybe even some long underwear! But I didn't know, so off I went, (almost) as naked as the day I was born. Brrrrrr!

Of course, we ended up risking our lives again. Thinking about it, though, I can honestly say that this time was actually worth it. You don't believe me? Well, keep reading, and I'll tell you what happened.

Chapter 1

Up Too Early

Nothing in the world could have kept Mr. Silver from attending Fogville's Fall Festival. And he insisted that the rest of the family couldn't miss it either. So on the morning of the festival, he dragged us all out of bed at dawn. He was determined that we would be the first ones to arrive.

"Come on, kids! We're going to be late!" Mr. Silver called as he hopped on one foot, trying to put his shoes on.

Moving like zombies, Michael, Becca, Tyler, and I wandered around the house. I was especially tired — bats like to sleep during the day, you know!

"Mom, do we really have to go?" Becca whined as we got ready to leave the house. I was hidden away in her backpack as usual.

"Come on, kids," Mrs. Silver replied. "You know it means a lot to your father."

When we finally stepped outside, the crisp morning air immediately woke us up.

"This is the

perfect day for the Fall Festival!" Mr. Silver said happily. "I can't wait to get there!"

The whole family climbed into the car to drive to the Fall Festival. It was being held just outside of the city in a large park. That was the only place big enough for the hundreds of visitors that came from Fogville's neighboring towns to attend every year.

The festival was already busy when we arrived. There were people and tents everywhere. From my spot inside Becca's backpack, it looked like a circus! I was more than happy to stay hidden inside, where it was comfy and warm.

The crowd pushed us along, and soon we arrived at the magnificent Villa Charlotte at the center of the park. It had originally been the home of a wealthy family but was later converted into a museum.

Michael immediately started giving us a lecture on its history. "Did you know that Villa Charlotte was originally designed as a home for the famous La Trippe family?" he said. "It was named after the La Trippes' daughter, Charlotte. That's her statue out front."

"Jeez, check out the nose on that girl!" Tyler

said as we walked up to the statue. "It looks like a beak!"

Out of the blue, a little girl wearing a fancy dress appeared. "Excuse me!" she snapped. "How dare you insult my great-great grandmother?"

"What do you mean, your great-great grandmother?" Tyler asked.

The girl rolled her eyes. "I'm not surprised you don't know what I'm talking about," she said. "Nobility isn't something you can learn. You have to be born with it. It's in your blood."

"Listen," Tyler retorted, "I don't know what's in your blood, but I'm pretty sure I know what's in your head — monkeys!"

"How rude!" the little girl exclaimed. "Do you know who you are talking to? I am Countess Violet La Trippe, and this is my ancestors' home."

Michael tried to put a stop to the argument.

"Please excuse my brother," Michael said. "He's always kidding around. I'm sure he didn't mean to offend you."

Violet eyed Michael from head to toe,

then held her hand out toward him. Michael kissed it lightly.

"I accept your apologies," the countess muttered, staring off into the distance. Then she walked off without a backward glance.

"Yuck! That was gross!" Tyler said. "Now you kiss strangers' hands? You'd better wash your lips!"

"Maybe you don't get it, but that stranger is a countess," Michael said.

"All I got was that you fell for some stuck-up brat!" Becca said.

The discussion was suddenly interrupted by Mr. Silver, who reappeared holding a huge cloud of cotton candy in his right hand. "Quick, kids!" he said. "Come and see!"

Chapter 2

Runaway Balloon!

We followed Mr. Silver to a huge red-and-yellow hot-air balloon that was tethered to the ground by a thick safety rope. The large wicker basket below it was floating five or six feet above the ground. It looked like an animal held on a leash, ready to break free at the first opportunity!

A thin man with a thick black mustache was inviting people to go for an exciting trip through the skies above Fogville.

"Step right up, ladies and gentlemen!" he called. "Take to the skies and experience an unforgettable one-hour trip above your town's rooftops! What are you waiting for?"

"Wow, that's cool!" Tyler exclaimed.

"What do you think, kids?" Mr. Silver asked, grinning. "Would you like to go for a ride?"

"I don't know. It's pretty expensive, Dad," Becca replied, looking at the price list.

"Oh, nonsense!" her father replied. He pulled out his wallet and walked up to the man. "Three tickets for my kids, please!"

I realized they were planning to take me just seconds before Becca began to climb into the basket of that flying contraption. I quickly slipped out of her backpack and hid in Mrs. Silver's arms.

"What's the matter, Echo?" Becca asked, laughing. "Are you afraid of flying?"

How on earth could a bat like me be afraid of flying!? I just didn't trust something that depended on a big stomach full of air instead of wings to fly! On top of that, I had a strange feeling in my stomach. Like my uncle Asclepius always used to say, "If your ears burn, it's okay to be concerned!"

Becca gave me a puzzled look. I smiled at her and fluttered my wings. "Of course I'm not afraid," I replied. "But I can go anywhere I want with these!"

"Bear with me just a little longer," the pilot said as soon as the Silver kids climbed a short rope ladder and stepped into the basket. "We'll take off as soon as we have a full house."

Tyler leaned over the edge of the basket and made funny faces at me while they waited. Then he made such a horrible one that I almost burst out laughing.

But Tyler wasn't joking around anymore.

He'd just seen the next passenger approaching the hot-air balloon.

I bet you already know who it was, don't you? You're right, it was Countess Violet La Trippe herself.

"Oh, no!" Tyler groaned. "Not her!"

"What are those three doing in my balloon?" Violet demanded. She glared at my friends like they were something that had gotten stuck to the bottom of her fancy shoe.

"Wait a minute! We were here first!" Becca replied angrily.

"Come on, Violet," the man with her coaxed. He appeared to be some kind of butler. "They look like nice children."

"Nice?" Violet repeated incredulously. "They were hardly nice to me outside Villa Charlotte earlier! I caught them making fun of my ancestors!"

"Please, Countess," Michael interrupted. "Come up. My brother won't bother you."

Violet smiled. "All right then, if I must," she said. "Will you help me up, please, Paul?"

The butler, Paul, put his hands together and made a step to help Violet up to the ladder. As Violet made her way into the basket, the pilot began untying the thick rope and removing the weights hanging along the outside of the basket.

That's when things really got crazy!

The countess missed the last step on the ladder and fell backward, slamming right into Paul as he tried to help her. Paul lost his balance and toppled backward into the pilot. The pilot dropped the safety rope before he

could get on board! It was like watching a bunch of dominoes!

The pilot tried to run after the balloon, but it quickly took off with my friends inside! The terrified countess clung to the rope ladder on the side, screaming her head off.

Everyone else started screaming too. The butler, the pilot, Mr. Silver, and even the small group of people that had gathered to watch the balloon take off.

Only Mrs. Silver stayed calm. She looked right at me and said: "Bring them back to me, Echo! Please!"

Can you picture a rocket on its launch pad, ready to go? You can? Well, I was faster than that.

Chapter 3

Driving Lessons

My heart felt like it was going to beat right out of my chest as I flew after my friends. As I watched, the Silver kids tried to pull the countess inside the basket of the quickly rising balloon.

Tyler and Becca gripped Michael's legs firmly as he hung upside down over the ladder. He managed to talk Violet into giving him her hand. "Don't look down!" I heard him yell as he pulled her inside. I breathed a sigh of relief when they were all on board safe and sound.

By the time I got there, the countess was in tears. "I knew I shouldn't have come on board with the three of you!" she yelled. "I knew it! Royalty should never mingle with commoners!"

"Well, it looks like us commoners just saved your life!" Becca reminded her. But it didn't make a difference. The countess just kept sobbing uncontrollably.

"Welcome aboard, Echo!" Tyler yelled as I landed on the edge of the basket. "I knew you couldn't resist the thrill of a hot-air balloon ride."

"Argh!" the countess shrieked. "What is that thing?"

"Are you talking to me?" I asked. "I'm a bat, of course. A *bat sapiens*, to be precise. I'm also a close friend of these three."

"Oh, I must have hit my head!" Violet

sobbed. "I hear animals talking! Somebody help me!"

It took all our patience to calm her down and convince her that she wasn't going crazy. Nevertheless, when I tried to kiss her hand in greeting, she started screaming all over again.

"Okay, enough's enough!" Becca yelled. "We've wasted enough time on her. Does anybody know how this thing works?"

We all turned to Michael, our walking encyclopedia.

"Hot-air balloons work because the hot air inside the balloon is lighter than the cold air around it. That's what pushes the balloon upward, like this," Michael said. He turned the burner handle and increased the flame that warmed the air inside the balloon. The balloon soared higher, and Violet yelped again.

"If you cool the air inside the balloon, it'll go down," Michael continued. "Like this." He tried to turn the handle the opposite direction, but it didn't budge.

"Uhhh . . ." Michael said, pushing the handle as hard as he could. "I think it's sort of . . . it might be just a little bit . . . well . . . stuck."

"Stuck?" the countess repeated. "What do you mean stuck?"

"That means we can't get back down and land!" Becca snapped.

"We can still reverse it, can't we?" Tyler asked. "We just need to get back to Fogville, and then someone will pull us down! How do you turn the wheel on this thing?"

"Well, actually," Michael said, looking at the rapidly shrinking town below us, "um . . . I don't think we can."

"What?" Violet squealed, her eyes wide with shock. "You mean you can't even take us

back? Change the course and bring me back home IMMEDIATELY! That's an order!"

"I would love to, Countess, but there's nothing I can do," Michael said. Just then, a violent gust of wind hit the hot-air balloon, sending it spinning out of control. We all jumped into each others' arms and huddled together in the center of the basket.

As we clung together helplessly, the hot-air balloon sailed into a thick blanket of dark, menacing clouds, and we lost our way completely.

Chapter 4

Heading North

All we could see was a thick layer of white fog. The temperature was dropping rapidly.

"I think we must be heading north," Michael said after another unsuccessful attempt at landing. "It's getting colder by the minute."

As I looked at Michael, his glasses fogged up before my eyes. I gulped. I just hoped it was due to the cold, rather than a signal of approaching trouble, like usual.

Next to me, Countess La Trippe shivered. Her fancy white party dress was no match for the cold air. She huddled on the floor of the basket and covered her shoulders with a filthy-looking blanket to avoid turning into a Popsicle. The countess was starting to look more like a pile of clothes than a little girl!

"Hey, check this out!" Tyler exclaimed suddenly. He was digging through a box he had found. "There are some hats and gloves in here! They must have put them here for the passengers. There's a jacket, too. Would you like it, Violet?" he asked.

Violet snatched the jacket from Tyler's hands and put it on without saying a word.

My friends were already dressed warmly, but they each grabbed a wool hat from the box and put it on their heads. I had to make do with a purple hat that went all the way down to my feet. I slipped back into Becca's backpack to try to stay warm.

Just then, Tyler remembered he that he still had his cell phone in his pocket. He pulled it out and called his parents.

"Hello? Hello, Mom?" he said, pressing the phone close to his ear. "It's Tyler. Yes, we're all okay. Um . . . I don't know. We're flying toward . . . I don't know where. Hello? Hello?"

He looked at the phone, then at all of us. "I think the battery's dead," he said apologetically.

Once again, the countess burst into tears.

"I can't take much more of her crying!" Becca complained.

"Well, I know something that would make us all feel better," Tyler said, grabbing his backpack. "How about a snack?"

"You brought food with you?" Becca asked.

"Of course I did!" Tyler replied. He pulled out a picnic basket. "I always like to be prepared. Just in case."

For once, we were grateful that Tyler had thought to bring a snack with him. The picnic basket was full of bread, cheese, sausage, crackers, peanut butter, apples, pretzels, cookies, water, and chewing gum.

Everyone dug in and grabbed something to eat. We were just starting to feel a little better when we were hit by another icy gust of wind. I shivered. It felt like a snowstorm was coming!

Suddenly the wind gusted so hard that it blew out the burner flame. We were done for!

Without the flame to keep it in the air, the balloon quickly started losing altitude. We spun around, out of control in the wind.

Michael worked up his courage and leaned over the edge of the basket to figure out where we were headed. His eyes widened with alarm. "We're landing!" he yelled.

Seconds later, the balloon hit the ground. Luckily, the impact wasn't too violent. The basket was tipped over on its side, and the red-and-yellow balloon deflated and fell on top of us, covering us completely.

Beneath my wings, I could feel something cold and powdery. It must have broken our fall. Opening my eyes, I realized that it was snow!

Chapter 5

A Living Avalanche!

I was the first to peek my head out from under the deflated balloon. Then, one by one, the worried faces of my travel companions appeared next to me.

As soon as we stuck our heads outside, however, we discovered that the snowstorm was in full swing! We quickly followed Michael's suggestion to seek cover under the balloon.

"Where are we?" the countess whined. "I want to go home!"

"I'm sure we'll be fine, Violet," Michael said, trying to reassure her. He glanced at the rest of us. "We've been in worse situations than this and always made it out okay. Right, guys?"

We all knew that that wasn't exactly the truth, but no one argued. We didn't want to hear the countess get worked up all over again.

"We'll wait for the storm to die down a little, and then we'll go looking for help," Michael added, keeping his cool.

We stayed hidden beneath the shelter of the balloon and listened to the wind blowing furiously outside. We had to hold the balloon down with our hands to keep it from flying off.

Luckily for us, the storm didn't last long. We were soon able to take a peek outside. We had landed in a beautiful valley, surrounded by thick trees and high mountains covered in snow.

"What now?" Tyler asked, hopping back and forth on his freezing feet.

Michael pointed at something near the bottom of the valley. "Look!" he said. "I could be wrong, but that looks like smoke to me."

We all looked where he pointed. It was true. Gray smoke was rising from behind a rocky ridge.

"We're saved!" Tyler shouted, overcome with

excitement. His voice echoed throughout the valley and was followed by a menacing rumble.

"Shut up!" Michael scolded him. "Don't you know you're not supposed to scream in the mountains? You might cause an avalanche!"

"I'm sorry!" Tyler whispered in apology. "I didn't know!"

"Echo," Michael started to ask me, "would you mind . . ."

". . . going down there to take a look?" I finished for him. "I'll go, I'll go! It's always me, every time, isn't it?!"

I took off and headed toward where the smoke was coming from. *At least flying will warm me up a bit,* I thought. *And keep my wings from freezing off!*

As I flew off to investigate, the Silver kids

rolled up the balloon and stuffed it in the basket.

"We should probably take it with us," Michael said. "We might need it."

Turning to Violet, Michael asked, "Do you want to sit in the basket? You'll stay warmer. And dry."

"Thank you," she said, sounding polite for the first time. "But I wouldn't want your brother and sister to be mad at me."

"Oh, don't worry," Michael said, smiling. "I'm sure my brother will be happy to push you. Won't you, Tyler?"

"Oh, sure," Tyler said sarcastically. "I can hardly wait." He placed his hands on the edge of the basket. "Hold tight, Countess. You're about to travel at the speed of light!"

Michael didn't even have time to warn him before the basket slipped on the snow. It instantly picked up speed, dragging a terrified Tyler behind it. Behind them, an avalanche started rumbling down the mountain, ready to sweep them away! There was no time to waste!

Fortunately, I had already found an opening in the rocks. That's where the smoke was coming from. As soon as the basket, which was holding Violet and dragging Michael, Tyler, and Becca, crashed into a snow bank near me, I frantically pointed to the opening. "This way, quick!" I yelled. "Get in there!"

The huge avalanche was bearing down on us, but the opening in the rocks was too narrow for it to filter through. The five of us crawled in as the snow thundered past above us.

Chapter 6

A Secret Cave

"Well, at least we won't freeze to death in here," Becca commented, moving closer to the fire in the middle of the cave.

A cave. You read that right. And an inhabited one, as far as we could tell. After all, someone must have started the fire that we were all keeping warm around. The fire wasn't our only clue. The cave also contained wooden tools, ropes, and snowshoes. We figured they had to belong to someone. But there was no living soul to be found.

"Look," Becca said. "There's a bed here too!"

"And there's some cheese over here!" Tyler mumbled with his mouth full. "It's delicious!"

"Put it down, Tyler!" Michael said. "That stuff's not yours!"

"What should we do?" Becca asked.

"Well, I don't think we have much of a choice," Michael said. "We'll wait 'til the people who live here come back, and then we'll tell them why we're here. Hopefully they'll be able to help us."

"And hopefully they're friendly!" I added.

"What do you mean, Echo?" Tyler asked, still snacking on the cheese he'd found.

"It's just that the old librarian I used to live with told me a story about a guy named Ulysses," I said. "He and his friends ended up in a similar situation. They ventured into the cave of an enormous Cyclops. From what I remember of the story, the giant almost ate them all up!"

"I don't want to get eaten up by a giant!" Tyler exclaimed, dropping the cheese.

"Calm down!" Michael said. "It's just a story. Besides, this guy can't be a giant. Look at his wooden spoon. It's only a little bit bigger than normal."

"Yeah, but look at his shoes!" Becca said. She held up a huge fur boot.

Violet was so terrified that she fainted right then and there. Michael tried to revive her as I flew up to the dark ceiling of the cave.

Tyler had no interest in hanging around. "Let's get out of here — now!" he said.

"And go where exactly?" Michael asked. "Outside to freeze to death?"

"Freezing is better than being someone's dinner," Tyler argued.

"Oh, knock it off, Tyler. You know Michael's right. We can't go outside," Becca said. She held up an old book with the words *Ice Age Fossils* written clearly across the cover. "Besides, a guy who reads stuff like this can't be that evil."

"Interesting . . ." Michael said. It seemed like he was going to say something else, but just then the countess started to wake up.

We tried to pass the time gathered around the fire. Michael started telling us one of Edgar Allan Poultry's tales, *The Return of the Yeti*. It was so scary that Violet almost fainted again.

Suddenly, a terrifying roar startled us. A huge shadow appeared inside the cave, and we could hear a clearly human voice making low, throaty noises.

"That's n-not the Y-Yeti, is it?" Tyler stuttered, looking terrified.

Whatever it was was getting closer. Michael leaned over and whispered to me. "Get ready, Echo. If the situation gets dangerous, fly out of here and look for help."

I nodded. I didn't want to leave my friends,

but I knew it was the best plan. I flew back up to the ceiling and waited for our guest to come in.

What I saw was some kind of caveman. He was covered in thick, bulky fur and had long hair and a scruffy beard.

As soon as he realized that there were people in his cave, he stared at my friends with a crazed expression on his face and let out a terrifying *ROAR!*

Michael glanced at me. That was the signal.

Less than a second later, I was in flight and on my way to find help for my friends.

Chapter 7

The Art of Eavesdropping

I flapped my numb wings as fast as I could as I took off in search of help. I couldn't stop thinking about my poor friends, stuck dealing with Mr. Neanderthal! He could be eating them for dinner, for all I knew. I had to hurry!

Thankfully, luck was on my side. I soon came across a group of tents gathered in a circle around an antenna not too far from the cave. There was a light shining inside the biggest one. There was definitely someone in there!

Once my enthusiasm was gone, though, I realized that I couldn't just land among those strangers and casually say, "Hello, everybody! I'm a talking bat, and I need your help freeing my friends from a caveman who lives just down the block. Could you give me a hand?"

I chose a more careful strategy and landed next to the brightly lit tent. I tiptoed closer to the window. Then, pricking up my half-frozen ears, I listened to what the people inside were saying.

"I'm telling you I heard it, Jordan!" someone said. "It must have been around eleven."

"Hearing it isn't enough!" another man said. "I need you to find it! Four hunters armed to the teeth with infrared binoculars and thermographs, and you're telling me you can't find a guy who's the size of an eighteen wheeler?"

"I'm sure it was him!" the first man replied. "I recognized him, I'm telling you. I even heard some . . . no, forget it. You wouldn't believe me anyway."

"Oh, c'mon. Don't be afraid! What else did you hear?" the second man asked.

"I heard voices," the first man said. "They sounded like kids' voices."

My little heart skipped a beat! What kids was that guy talking about?

"Well, that's great. You're hallucinating now!" said Jordan, the guy I figured had to be the boss. "Listen to me, and listen carefully. If we don't find and kill that animal in the next three days, we'll blow the deal of the century. Do you know how much a fur like that is worth?"

"Don't tell me, boss," the other man replied. "I don't want to know."

"Then you'd better get back out there until it's dark, and shoot everything that moves! I want that beast! And I want its fur! Now! Do I make myself clear?!"

What's the big deal about this fur? I wondered. And what animal are they talking about?

Suddenly three men, all covered from head to toe in thick orange snowsuits, burst out of the tent. They were all wearing mirrored glasses and carrying huge rifles. Mumbling under their breath, the men jogged away from the camp. Luckily they were headed in the opposite direction of the cave where I'd left my friends.

I knew one thing for certain — I wasn't going to get any help from these people. I was lucky I didn't have fur, or they'd probably be after me!

I felt very sorry for the poor animal they were after. I would have done everything to warn him. Unfortunately, all I could do for the time being was to go back to the cave and tell my friends what I'd overheard.

Hopefully I would find them still in one piece.

Chapter 8

The Spirit of the Mountain

Only my trusty sense of direction kept me from getting lost in that vast, white landscape. Everything looked exactly the same! Luckily, I spotted the familiar wisp of smoke coming from the cave and used it as a compass.

When I arrived, I hung upside down in front of cave entrance and tried to peek in. The Neanderthal was broiling something on a spit. My friends were lying next to the wall, trussed up like chickens but safe and sound. I sighed in relief.

It was up to me to set them free. My problem, however, was always the same. How was I going to defeat an opponent so much bigger and stronger than me? Using my brains, of course!

With a slight flapping of my wings, I entered the cave unseen and stopped right above the fire. Becca saw me immediately, but didn't say anything.

Using one of the tricks I had learned from my cousin Limp Wing, member of the Aerobatic Display Team, I performed the "Winged Bullhorn."

I steadied my grip on the ceiling, put my wings around my mouth like a funnel, and in

the lowest voice I could manage, said, "What
are you doing to my friends-ends-ends. . . ."
There was even an echo! It couldn't get better
than that!

"Who's that?" the caveman asked. He stood
up, looking terrified. "What's going on?"

Even Michael and Tyler looked startled, not to
mention Violet, who looked downright terrified.
Becca, on the other hand, was giggling.

"I am the spirit of the mountain-ountain-ountain. . . ." I went on. "Let those children go immediately, or you will regret it-it-it-it-it. . . ."

"What if I don't?" the caveman demanded, regaining some of his courage. "What are you going to do? Huh?"

I said the first thing that popped into my head. "I will call the poachers that have been wandering around here-ere-ere. . . ."

"Poachers? Are you serious?" he asked, sounding scared. He kept looking around as he tried to figure out where the voice was coming from.

"Of course I am," I insisted. "There are four of them, and they have rifles as big as cannons-annons-annons. . . ."

"That means Ursula is in danger!" the man cried, running toward the wall and reaching for a big horn.

He went over to the exit and blew into it with all his power. *BOOOOOOOOO!*

The sound echoed throughout the valley. The walls of the cave started shaking so violently that I lost my grip and fell down. Luckily I landed on the man's back and bounced onto the floor of the cave rather than falling straight into the fire!

The caveman turned around, looking as annoyed as if he had been stung by a mosquito. When he saw me lying half-conscious on the floor, he picked me up with his big hand, brought me close to his face, and said, "Who exactly are you supposed to be?"

"I, uh . . . I'm the spirit of the mountain," I said in a faint voice. "I order you to release my friends . . . please."

The caveman burst into laughter, but quickly turned serious again. Unfazed by the fact that he was talking to a bat, he asked me again, "Did you really see the poachers?"

"Yes, sir," I said. "They said they were looking for a large fur animal."

The man flinched. Then he turned his back to us and looked toward the entrance to the cave. "Hold on to something," he warned us. "She's coming."

Chapter 9

The Glowing Roll

At first, the earth rumbled. Then, something
outside the cave started ramming into the
entrance wall. It was so violent that the whole
left arch started shaking and collapsed.

As soon as the dust had settled, we saw what
had caused the damage. A huge, dark shadow
bounced forward to the center of the cave, and
came to a stop in front of the fire.

My friends and I pressed our backs against
the wall in absolute horror. Before us stood the

biggest, hairiest elephant I'd ever seen! Its two tusks were as sharp as spears! And it looked pretty mad!

The caveman walked up to the creature and started petting it like it was a little lap dog. "Easy, Ursula, these children aren't going to hurt you!" he softly whispered in its ear.

"What . . . what is . . . that?" stuttered Tyler, who had turned as white as a ghost.

"This? It's a mammoth, of course," the man replied. "Haven't you ever seen a picture of a mammoth before?"

"Well, of course!" Michael replied excitedly. "But I thought they went extinct after the last ice age."

"That's what I used to think too. Before I explored these remote valleys, that is," the caveman said, smiling at Ursula. "Then I met Ursula and changed my mind. For a long time, I was the only one who knew about her, but someone must have seen her. Now those poachers are after her."

The enormous mammoth blew an angry puff of air out its nose, raising a big cloud of dust inside the cave. It seemed she didn't think much of the poachers either.

"Why are they looking for her?" Becca asked.

I could see the concern on her face. Becca loves all animals, no matter how big or how small!

"Because they want her fur," the caveman told us. "A fur like hers is worth a lot of money."

Suddenly the caveman sprang into action. "They're coming! I must be quick!" he exclaimed. He started piling up snow in front of the cave's entrance, desperately trying to barricade us inside.

"Let us go!" Michael exclaimed from his spot on the floor. "We can help you!"

"Forget it." The man rudely shooed him away. "You kids would just slow me down."

"You'll never close off the cave in time on your own!" Michael insisted. "You need us!"

The man stopped and turned to face his prisoners. While he was untying the ropes he had trussed them with, he said threateningly, "If this is a joke, it'll cost you dearly!"

Just then, we heard several shots outside the cave.

"They're already here!" the caveman cried desperately. "They must have heard the horn! Oh, I was a fool to use it!"

"It's not over yet!" Michael said. "Come here, Echo! I have an idea."

As usual, Michael's idea was both clever and effective. Too bad I was the one who had to put it into action.

"You're the only one who can get to the top of the mountain quickly enough," Michael explained. "Once you get to the top, all you have to do is . . ."

"Stop! That's enough!" I interrupted him. I didn't need any further explanation. I knew exactly what I had to do. I just had to apply another one of Limp Wing's lessons — The Glowing Roll.

What's the point of the Glowing Roll, you ask? It's simple! You use it to cause an avalanche, starting with just a tiny snowball. It works even better if the snowball contains a brave (and slightly crazy) rolling bat!

Let me make this story short for you. When

I reached the top of the mountain, I took a deep breath and started rolling down the mountainside. Brrrr! It was freezing! As I rolled, more and more snow gathered around me until I was at the center of a giant snowball.

I raced down the hill until the snowball came to a sudden stop as it crashed into the front of

the cave. The snowball that had formed was so huge that it blocked the entrance completely.

The group of poachers, led by two big dogs, arrived just a moment later. When they discovered the only entrance to the cave was blocked, they were furious. They were so angry at having blown their chance to capture their prey that they started shooting into the air.

Fortunately, they didn't realize I was spying on them from behind a mound of collapsed snow. Ursula and my friends were safe. I was so proud!

That is, until I realized that they were all still safe inside the cave . . . and I wasn't!

Chapter 10

Quite Alive For a Dead Man

The poachers went back to their camp to get a couple of shovels so they could start digging. They left their dogs behind to guard the entrance to the cave in the meantime.

I had to get out of there as soon as possible! I tried to break free of the snowball I'd created, but I realized that I was stuck. My legs were trapped in the ice. And one of those ugly dogs was headed straight for me! Scaredy-bat! What now?

I didn't know it at the time, but that's the exact same thing the people inside the cave were wondering.

"Well done, kids!" the Neanderthal said. "Thanks to you, Ursula is safe! At least for now."

"Yeah," Tyler said. "But thanks to us, now we're trapped! And those poachers are out there already trying to get in!"

"I can't believe you didn't design an emergency exit," Violet said. "You . . . you . . . you do have a name, right?"

"I used to," the man replied, taking a seat on the floor of the cave. He pulled out a pair of small, round glasses and put them on. "When I was a professor my name was Fred Ventura."

"You were a professor?" Tyler asked, sounding shocked. "Where? What were you teaching? Beardology 101?"

"Paleontology," the caveman replied. "Studying fossils has always been my passion."

"Of course! I remember now!" Michael exclaimed. "Fred Ventura! The greatest mammoth researcher of the twentieth century! You wrote *Find Fossils in Your Backyard* and *How to Housebreak a Dinosaur*. I loved your books when I was in grade school!

When you went missing, the story was in practically every newspaper. Everyone thought you were dead!"

FRED VENTURA
Find Fossils in Your Backyard

VENTURA
ow to
Housebreak
a Dinosaur

"I did everything I could to make people believe that," Professor Ventura explained. "Once I found Ursula, I tried to keep her existence a secret to protect her. As you can see, I unfortunately failed."

"Don't say that, Professor," Michael encouraged him. "There's still hope!"

The professor shook his head sadly. "You kids need to start thinking about how to get out of here and save yourselves. Ursula and I will stay here. We'll fight this final battle together! Am I right, old friend?"

Standing next to the fire, the mammoth shook its head.

"Isn't she afraid?" Becca asked. "I thought most animals were afraid of fire."

"Only silly animals," the professor said. "I taught Ursula that fire keeps us warm, and that it isn't dangerous as long as she doesn't get too close. Every night, she comes up to the entrance of the cave to warm up with her . . . um . . . never mind. Come on, Ursula! Let's get ready to give those poachers a good fight!"

Apparently Ursula understood what the professor said, because she let out a deep breath, stepped back a couple of feet, and then charged toward the far side of the cave.

Violet pulled Michael closer and clung to his

arm while Tyler covered his ears against the deafening noise.

After Ursula's third charge, the rock wall collapsed. Behind it was a long stone corridor that seemed to lead into the center of the mountain.

The hunters, who had just returned with shovels, heard Ursula demolishing the wall. "That beast must be nervous," they said happily. "It knows there's no way out!"

Back inside the cave, the professor used the fire to light a big torch and gestured for the kids to follow him.

Chapter 11

So Long, Suckers!

I was still trapped outside as all of this was happening, and I had just been spotted by a huge, angry dog. I was sure I was about to end up as that dog's chew toy! I was so nervous that

I started sweating. That's what saved me! It was enough to melt away the layer of ice I was trapped in.

That mutt was almost on top of me when I burst out of the snow and fluttered away from under its nose. It started barking furiously, drawing the men's attention.

"Take a look at that!" one of them shouted. "It's an arctic bat!"

I would have forgiven the fact that they didn't know bats don't live in the arctic, but did those hunters really have to shoot at me?

I immediately became a flying target. By golly! Fortunately, those guys were terrible shots, and a couple of them hit the mountain instead of me. What happened then? Another disastrous avalanche!

I immediately soared high in the air, well

above the rushing snow beneath. Back on the ground, the poachers and their dogs were buried under two feet of snow.

Serves them right! I thought. *I hope they'll learn from this experience, but I also hope they all get out of there alive!* Well, you know, I'm a kind-hearted bat!

The dogs were the first to crawl out of the snow. Once they were free, they got to work rescuing their numb, but very-much-alive, masters.

I was just about to scoot when I saw a still-half-covered Jordan point to the mountainside with a bewildered look on his face. "There! Look over there!" he yelled.

Men and dogs alike turned to look at where he'd been pointing. I couldn't help my curiosity and turned to look as well, completely forgetting about flying away.

By my grandpa's sonar! Was I really seeing that, or was it some kind of snow-induced hallucination? Maybe my mind was playing tricks on me. After all, it's not every day you see a perfectly preserved mammoth frozen in the ice!

"Hey, boss!" one of the men yelled. "There's the fur we've been looking for! We didn't even need to waste our ammo on it! What do you think?"

"I think your brain must be the size of a ping-pong ball!" Jordan scolded him. "Forget about the fur! Don't you understand that this might be the most important discovery of the century? Museums will be ready to pay truckloads of money for this big guy! We're gonna be rich and famous!"

"Famous?" the other hunter repeated. "Whoa! I like the sound of that!"

"Aren't we going to look for the other mammoth anymore?" another one asked.

"Not for the time being. Go back to the campsite and radio a request to the others. I want them to send a helicopter with a large loading net. What are you looking at?" he asked me, spotting me still fluttering nearby. "You're not waiting for a tip, are ya?"

Grrr! That made me so mad! Who did he think I was? A poacher?

With the corner of my eye, I noticed that the avalanche had opened a small hole in front of the cave. I quickly decided that it was time to go find my friends. Before I entered the cave, though, I took a moment to stick my tongue out at the poachers and blow Jordan and his crew a loud raspberry!

Chapter 12

Mice and Elephants

I noticed the new tunnel as soon as I entered the cave. It was pretty hard to miss. *Whoa!* I thought. *Who on earth did that? And more importantly, where does the tunnel lead?*

Deep inside, I knew it must lead to my friends. So, trusting my sonar, I dashed into that dark tunnel. I ducked pointed rocks, grazed frozen walls, and overcame chilly gusts of air. Finally, I saw a dim light at the end of the tunnel and recognized Tyler's voice.

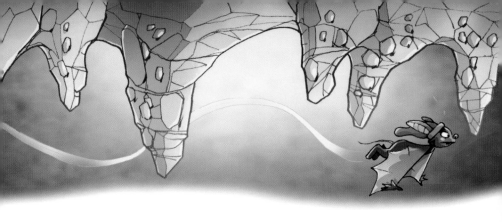

"I knew we shouldn't trust a hairy elephant!" he complained. "Would someone please tell me where we're going."

"Don't worry, Tyler," Becca reassured him. "Ursula knows what she's doing. Isn't that right, Professor?"

"I think so," the professor answered. "Or at least I hope she does."

When my friends spotted me approaching they were thrilled. Most of them, at least.

"Echo!" Tyler exclaimed. "Thank goodness you're here! I knew you would make it!"

But no one had anticipated the effect I would have on the mammoth. Ursula started trumpeting in terror as soon as she saw me!

"What's wrong with her?" Tyler asked. "Is she cold again?"

"Hide the bat! Quick!" Professor Ventura screamed, trying to calm Ursula down.

Have you heard the rumor that elephants are afraid of mice? Well, the same apparently goes for mammoths. I can't say that I blame Ursula for panicking. I was scared wingless of that wild thing myself!

Tyler grabbed me and put me away in his jacket. Violet, who had turned pale with fear, was glued to Michael. Professor Ventura kept trying to calm her down, but Ursula wouldn't listen.

Can you guess who solved the situation? My girl Becca, of course! She really has a way with animals. She walked right up to Ursula and gently stroked the animal's trunk, talking to her soothingly. Ursula immediately calmed down. She even gently lifted Becca up and set her on her back.

"I've never seen anything like that!" an astonished Professor Ventura said. Then he regained his composure. He turned to Tyler. "Maybe your little bat friend can tell us what's going on outside the cave."

Still hiding out of sight inside Tyler's jacket, I told everyone what had happened in front of the cave. When I got to the part about finding the frozen mammoth, Professor Ventura looked upset.

"I knew it was there," he said, shaking his head sadly. "I always knew, but I never managed to find it. It must have been Ursula's mate and the father of . . . um . . . never mind. All that matters is that the poachers have stopped looking for us. Come on. We have to keep walking."

"Where to, exactly?" Tyler asked. "The center of the earth?"

"Trust Ursula," the professor told him. "She knows what she's doing."

We all followed the mammoth, which was still carrying Becca on its back. We squeezed through the tunnels inside the mountain until we discovered a serious obstacle in our way — an underground lake. It was half frozen, and walking around it was impossible.

"End of the line," Tyler said. The torch the professor had been carrying suddenly blew out. "And end of the light!"

There we were, deep inside the belly of a mountain, with a mammoth and an ex-professor dressed as a caveman. We were trapped, unable to go forward or back. Can you think of a worse situation to be in?

Chapter 13

Becca's Hidden Talent

Believe it or not, Becca and Michael were not at all worried. They loved adventures like this! Tyler and I, on the other hand, hated them with a passion.

One of the reasons why I hated them was because the solution to the problem usually involved me! This time was no exception.

"Tyler," Michael said to his brother, "do you have that portable light generator in your bag?"

"Of course," Tyler replied. "I always have my inventions with me. Why?"

"We need some light," Michael replied. He turned to me. "Echo, do you know if your sonar works underwater?"

"D-do I have to go in the water?" I stuttered.

"No, don't worry," Michael said. "I just need you to measure the depth of the lake."

Phew! Was that ever a relief! A short flight a few inches above the surface of the lake and I had an answer. "It think it's about 30 feet," I told Michael.

"Perfect," Michael replied, rubbing his hands together in anticipation. "We can do it."

By that time, Violet was looking at Michael the same way you admire the monument of an illustrious person.

"What are you thinking?" Professor Ventura asked.

"It's quite simple," Michael said. "Since the lake isn't too deep and elephants are very good swimmers, I thought we could all ride Ursula across the lake. What do you think?"

"I think it's a wonderful idea. Unfortunately, Ursula will never set foot into that icy water. She's not really a fan of the cold."

"I bet my sister could talk her into it," Michael said. "What do you think, Becca?"

"I could try," Becca replied from where she still sat on Ursula's back. She leaned forward and whispered something in the mammoth's right ear. At first the animal shook its head and turned its back to the lake. Becca hopped off its back and planted herself in front of the mammoth.

"Let it go, young lady," the professor told her. "When she gets like that, there's no point in trying to change her mind."

But Becca refused to give up. She stared into Ursula's eyes. "Come on, girl," Becca urged. "I know you don't want to, but it's the only way to get out of here. And it's also the only way to see him again. You know that."

"What is she talking about?" Professor

Ventura asked. He seemed as bewildered as we were by what Becca was saying.

Suddenly Ursula knelt on the ground and set her trunk against her side like a ladder.

"Come on, get up here!" Becca said with a grin. "It's time to go wading!"

We all scrambled up onto the mammoth's enormous back. (I stayed hidden inside Tyler's jacket). Then Ursula stood up and stepped into the crystal-clear water of the lake without a single whimper. It was an amazing experience!

When we got to the other side, the mammoth didn't stop to let us down. Instead, it actually picked up its pace.

"Easy, Ursula! Slow down!" the professor shouted. He seemed as scared as we were. Becca was the only one who was actually enjoying it.

By then the mammoth was actually galloping. I didn't even want to imagine what would happen if we came across something in our path. I wasn't sure she'd be able to stop!

Luckily, we didn't run into anything. As a matter of fact, a few hundred yards ahead, I could see a window of blinding light. It was a way out! We had reached the other side of the mountain.

Trumpeting powerfully, the mammoth stampeded outside, splashing snow all around.

We were finally outside!

Chapter 14

A Fake Finale

We were all so happy to be alive (and out of that cave!) that we were overcome with emotion. Professor Ventura hugged Becca, Becca hugged me, I hugged Violet, and Violet hugged Michael. His face immediately turned beet red.

Tyler didn't hug anyone. He was too focused on starting a furious snowball fight that involved everyone. Soon, snowballs were flying everywhere.

I tried to take part in it too, but the biggest snowballs I could throw were the size of cherries. I soon ended up buried in snow. *Brrrr! Why does this keep happening to me?* I wondered.

Ursula put an end to the snowball fight and brought us all back to reality when she suddenly trumpeted loudly. It sounded like she was calling to someone.

"Hey! She's shaking like a leaf!" the professor said worriedly. "I knew that the water was too cold for her!"

"Let's rub her with snow!" Michael suggested. "I read somewhere that even though snow is cold, that can help keep you warm."

Everyone (except me of course) got busy rubbing the animal with snow. She seemed to appreciate it. (Personally, I thought being rubbed with snow sounded like torture!)

Feeling visibly better, Ursula took a couple of steps away from us and let out a third cry. It echoed throughout the valley.

"What did you tell her when you whispered in her ear earlier?" Professor Ventura asked Becca. "Who was she supposed to see again?"

"Him," Becca said, pointing at the horizon. We all looked where she pointed and saw a small shape trotting across the snowy landscape toward Ursula. It was a beautiful baby mammoth!

"B . . . but," the professor stammered. "How did you know?"

Becca just shrugged and smiled. "Let's just say that we girls understand each other!" she said with a laugh.

* * *

That should have been a happy ending, right? Mother finds her child, everyone is safe and sound, and we all lived happily ever after. Not for us it wasn't!

As we watched the happy reunion between Ursula and her baby, my extremely sensitive ears picked up a noise. At first, I was the only one who could hear it. But one by one, the others picked up on it too. As it drew closer, we all recognized the sound.

"That's a helicopter!" Michael cried. "Quick, we have to find a hiding place!"

"Ursula!" Professor Ventura yelled like a madman. "Run, Ursula! They'll see you! You have to hide!"

But Ursula, who was still busy lovingly hugging her baby, didn't move an inch.

I looked up at the sky as the helicopter

approached. In the pilot's seat, I could see a
man wearing an orange snowsuit. That had to
be one of the poachers Jordan had ordered to
transport the frozen mammoth they had found
near the cave.

But if the poachers discovered Ursula and her
baby, they would forget all about that frozen
mammoth, I realized. After all, if they thought
a mammoth fossil would make them rich and
famous, imagine what two living, breathing

mammoths would do! We couldn't let them
see Ursula and her baby. There was no time to
waste!

Just then, an idea hit me. I knew exactly
what I needed to do. Squeaking, I zeroed in on
Ursula and her baby. Flapping my little wings
frantically, I fluttered threateningly around both
of them!

The effect was immediate. They were both

so terrified that they took off running, straight back into the tunnel under the mountain. My plan had worked!

The mammoths hid there, safe and sound, until the helicopter had disappeared back over the horizon.

None of the poachers ever knew Ursula and her baby were there.

Chapter 15

Family Reunion

I don't know if Professor Ventura had ever seen a hot-air balloon before. But it didn't matter. He helped us fix it by repairing the broken burner handle and refilling the balloon with hot air.

When the balloon was fixed, he was ready to watch us take off. But not before thanking us and saying goodbye to each person . . . and bat!

"Are you really sure you want to stay here?" Michael asked him.

"Of course I'm sure!" the professor replied. "Ursula and her baby still need me here. I couldn't leave them. You kids have a safe trip back!"

He was about to untie the mooring line when Ursula suddenly appeared with her baby by her side. They wanted to say goodbye too! I didn't want to scare them again, so I disappeared into Tyler's jacket.

Suddenly, I was grabbed by some kind of huge, hairy vacuum hose. Ursula was holding me in midair and staring at me threateningly. She seemed determined to make me pay for scaring her and her baby. Didn't she realize I'd only been trying to help?!

"Let him go, Ursula!" the professor shouted. "He's your friend too!"

But apparently Ursula already knew that. She placed me on her baby's back and patted me gently on the head. It seemed to be her way of saying, "Thanks! If it hadn't been for you, those men in the helicopter would have seen us and come after us!"

Phew! I didn't know if I felt like crying because I was so touched, or because I had just come extremely close to being someone's dinner!

We all finished saying our goodbyes and climbed into the hot-air balloon. That's when the unexpected happened.

Professor Ventura finished untying the mooring line, and stepped back to wave us off.

But as the balloon started to rise in the air, he
was thrown into the basket. Who had done it?
His mammoth, of course!

"Nooo! Ursula, nooo!" the professor cried
desperately, leaning over the edge of the basket.
"Why did you do that?"

If the mammoth had been able to speak,
I believe it would have said, "Go back home,
Professor! Go back to those who love you, and
tell them that you're still alive!"

* * *

Even though Professor Ventura was with us, the journey back to Fogville was worse than our first flight — and that's saying something!

We miraculously managed to keep the balloon inflated, but the violent winds tossed us left and right like a ship caught in the middle of a storm.

And our landing was a complete disaster! We crashed near a small village along the coast. Needless to say the people who lived there were pretty surprised to find a hot air balloon full of children crash landing in their town!

Luckily, our disappearance from Fogville's Fall Festival had been in most of the newspapers. Apparently Violet had been telling the truth — she really was a countess! And when you disappear with royalty, it's a pretty big deal.

Our sudden and mysterious reappearance was front-page news!

Mr. and Mrs. Silver had been searching for us frantically since the festival. They almost had a heart attack when they read in *The Fogville Echo* that we had been found.

As soon as word got out that Professor Ventura, the famous missing paleontologist, had been found with us, newspapers and TV networks around the world went crazy.

Reporters and onlookers swarmed us when we arrived at the Fogville Airport. It's a shame that I couldn't sign any autographs. It would have been the perfect opportunity to gain some publicity as a writer!

When we arrived, we also discovered that Professor Ventura had a son! I think Ursula somehow knew that, and that's why she sent him back with us. Mother's intuition, maybe! As soon as the professor saw his son, he grabbed him and hugged him tightly.

It turns out that in Professor Ventura's absence, his son had become a paleontologist too, just like his father. He researched the fossils of smaller animals like birds and reptiles.

I couldn't believe it! It turns out that Professor Ventura's son had even found the oldest fossil of a prehistoric bat.

The professor decided to hold a press conference to explain to the scientific world where he had been for all those years.

"I was trying to verify a theory I had regarding the possible survival of mammoths," Professor Ventura announced to the crowd of reporters that had gathered. "But I'm sorry to report that after all my years searching, I found absolutely no trace that mammoths still exist."

"What did this experience teach you?" a reporter asked.

"I've learned that even though adventure is exciting, it's nice to go back to the people who love us," the professor replied. "And that changing your interests every now and then is nice too."

Then Professor Ventura turned and winked at me. "That's why I'm making it official," he added. "From here on out, I'll be following my son's lead and studying smaller fossils, specifically those of bats. I've discovered that they are extremely fascinating animals."

* * *

Violet was very happy to meet Mr. and Mrs. Silver. It seemed our adventure had changed her whole attitude! Just before her parents arrived to pick her up, she said one of the nicest things my friends and I had ever heard. At least coming from her.

"You know," she said, "I never imagined that hanging out with commoners could actually be so much fun!"

Then she hugged us one by one. When it was Michael's turn, she gave him an extra-long hug. She even planted a kiss on his cheek before she turned to leave. Michael's face immediately turned bright red.

"Gross!" Tyler muttered, making a gagging face at his brother.

Becca started teasing Michael. "Violet and Michael, sitting in a tree," she whispered in a singsong voice. "K-I-S-S-I-N-G!"

But Michael simply ignored his brother and sister. It seemed even their teasing couldn't bring him down.

"I hope I'll see you again!" Violet called back to him as she climbed into her car. "Maybe at next year's Fall Festival."

"I hope so too, Countess La Trippe!" Michael replied, still blushing. "I can't wait!"

"Please, call me Violet," she replied, fluttering her long eyelashes.

* * *

Ever since we returned from our latest

adventure, Michael has been acting very differently. Strange, almost. He's been spending hour after hour lying on his bed and sighing. When he's not doing that, he's researching information on next year's Fall Festival.

And on his nightstand the other day, I found a very different book from the Edgar Alan Poultry horror tales he usually reads. It was called *The Handbook for Understanding Girls*.

What do you think? Could he have possibly fallen in love?!

A "prehistoric" goodbye from your friend,

Echo

ABOUT THE AUTHOR

Roberto Pavanello is an accomplished children's author and teacher. He currently teaches Italian at a local middle school and is an expert in children's theater. Pavanello has written many children's books, including *Dracula and the School of Vampires*, *Look I'm Calling the Shadow Man!*, and the Bat Pat series, which has been published in Spain, Belgium, Holland, Turkey, Brazil, Argentina, China, and now the United States as Echo and the Bat Pack. He is also the author of the Oscar & Co. series, as well as the Flambus Green books. Pavanello currently lives in Italy with his wife and three children.

GLOSSARY

barricade (BA-ruh-kade) — building walls or obstacles to stop someone from getting past a certain point

corridor (KOR-uh-dur) — a long hallway or passage

extinct (ek-STINGKT) — an animal that has died out

mammoth (MAM-uhth) — an extinct animal like a large elephant, with long, curved tusks and shaggy hair, that lived during the Ice Age

menacing (MEN-iss-ing) — something that is threatening or dangerous

paleontologist (pey-lee-uhn-TOL-uh-jist) — someone who studies fossils and other ancient life forms

prehistoric (pree-hi-STOR-ik) — belonging to a time before history was recorded in written form

trussed (truhst) — tied up

DISCUSSION QUESTIONS

1. Have you ever been on a hot-air balloon ride? Would you like to go on one? Talk about why or why not.

2. What do you think happened to Ursula and her baby after Professor Ventura, the Silver kids, and I left? Talk about some posssible scenarios.

3. Mammoths no longer exist because they went extinct. Talk about some other animals you know of that are extinct.

WRITING PROMPTS

1. Mr. Silver was so excited to go to Fogville's Fall Festival. Write about a time you went to a fair or festival. What kinds of attractions did you see?

2. Write about the difference between animals that are extinct and animals that are endangered. What are some ways to protect endangered animals?

3. Pretend that you're a reporter for the *Fogville Echo*. Write an article about Professor Ventura's return to civilization.

THE FUN DOESN'T STOP HERE!

Discover more:

Videos & Contests

Games & Puzzles

Heroes & Villains

Authors & Illustrators

www.capstonekids.com

Find cool websites and more books like this one at
www.facthound.com.
Just type in the Book ID: 9781434238351
and you're ready to go!